ANGY BANGY BOO
and MR SKADOC

Written by Heidi Balzer
Illustrated by Sarah Holliday

To the Parkin-Balzer friendships.

"Angus" is his given name - but since his mother's friend
called him "Angy Bangy Boo", no one uses the other.

In Angus' opinion, this nickname proved
the woman was clearly bonkers.

Angy Bangy Boo was a lonely boy
Aged 7 years 4 months and just 1 day.
It had been a long time from January to May.
(Most of that time was spent in the loo,
The thing that poor Angy most liked to do).
It was not that he needed a wee or a poo,
He just liked talking to Mr Skadoo:
A tiny, delightful, stuffed elephant shrew, who,
Lived all alone in the new downstairs loo.

Why, you may ask, would Angy B Boo
Need to converse with an elephant shrew?
Well, he needed a friend for he had lost two
When the family moved from Zim to Buccleuch.
To the land of grey skies, haggis and tattoos
(Tattoos with Scots pipe bands
not those his mother said "No!" to).

Mr Skadoo with his curious expression
Made you feel he was always ready to listen.
So Angy talked to the shrew,
And they talked through and through,
Of the land they both missed,
and the things they both knew.
Of groundnuts
and mealies roasted on fire,
Of great elephant herds
and of ants that were flyers,
And strangest of all,
how the sky there seemed higher.

Mum often said, "Angy, please get out of that loo!
Stop chatting to that silly old moth-eaten shrew!"
But if mum only knew that Mr Skadoo,
Was far more elephant than he was shrew.
And if disrespected, just what he might do,
Perhaps even bite off a toe or a few!

His mother said, "Angy, go out and enjoy
the proper Scottish weather",
"Just remember your coat and your wellies
and, of course, an umbrella!"

But he'd rather sit there
In the warm downstairs loo
Having a chat to Mr Skadoo.
About mad guava fights,
and long swims in the pool.
And so many things that Angy B Boo,
and his old Zimbo friends just wanted to do.

Angy B Boo did not feel like "outside",
Knee high in mud and maybe cow poo!
Talking to boring old heifers
that only say moo.
Besides which, you never could know
the mood of the coo.
Was it Highland or low?
And with all that hair,
you could not read its eyes
Would it give you a nice or a nasty surprise?

One day, Angy walked in the forest alone
with nothing to do, he was kicking a stone.
When out of the blue, he heard a voice say
"Is kicking stones around
some foreign game that you play?"

"My name is Callum and I'd like to play
At football, stone-kicking, or climbing up trees,
Whatever you please!
Whatever you like, I'll just park my bike.
I think I could do with a new friend like you.

Despite that abysmal old Scottish weather
The two boys had fun and did lots together.
They climbed up a cairn and sailed on a loch,
And tried their hand at tobogganing
Until they hit a big rock!

Callum showed Angus how to play conkers,
even though he thought the game was quite bonkers.
They had fights with pinecones, which hurt more than guavas
But were much less messy - so approved by their mothers.

As the boys' frienship grew, they even went to the zoo;
Where Callum saw animals Angus was used to.
With help from his new friend, Angy did, slowly;
Begin to feel better about moving to Buccleuch.
Although the Scots weather could still make him feel lowly.

As the weeks and months went by, Angy Bangy Boo
spent less of his time in the downstairs loo.

But while in there "on business" he caught up with Skadoo,
Sharing memories of Zim, that they both loved and knew.
They vowed that one day they'd return there together
To the place so imprinted upon them forever.

Printed in Great Britain
by Amazon